He Is Back To

Wildcats vs Mu

MW01180656

Wow! We are in for a very exciting finish as the Mustangs have just scored. The Wildcats are still winning 29 to 24 with only 3 minutes left in this championship football game. The fans are on the edge of their seats as the Mustangs are set to kick the ball to the Wildcats. Can the Wildcats hold on to the ball and their lead to win the game? Can the Mustangs get the ball back and score one more touchdown to win? Both teams are ready for the kick-off, so let's check out the action.

ISBN 978-0-9808866-2-7

Practice early reading skills using the special page format.
- see our Literacy Guide on page 54 -

Support the literacy development of all children.
www.boysRreading.com

ColorSports Publishing Inc.

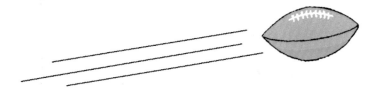

ColourSports Publishing Inc. - 5 Livingstone Dr. - Dundas - L9H 7S3 - Ontario - Canada

Printed in China

Welcome football fans, kids, parents, grammas and gramps.
Who will win this big game and be this year's new champs?

Will it be the Wildcats, wearing the yellow, white and Black?
They pounce on you quick and blitz the quarterback.

Or will the Mustangs win the game, by using their great speed.
Like red, white and blue horses, in a galloping stampede.

The Wildcats are winning now, twenty-nine to twenty-four.
The game time is running out, and the Mustangs need to score.

A a
B b
C c
D d
E e
F f
G g
H h
I i
J j
K k
L l
M m
N n
O o
P p
Q q
R r
S s
T t
U u
V v
W w
X x
Y y
Z z

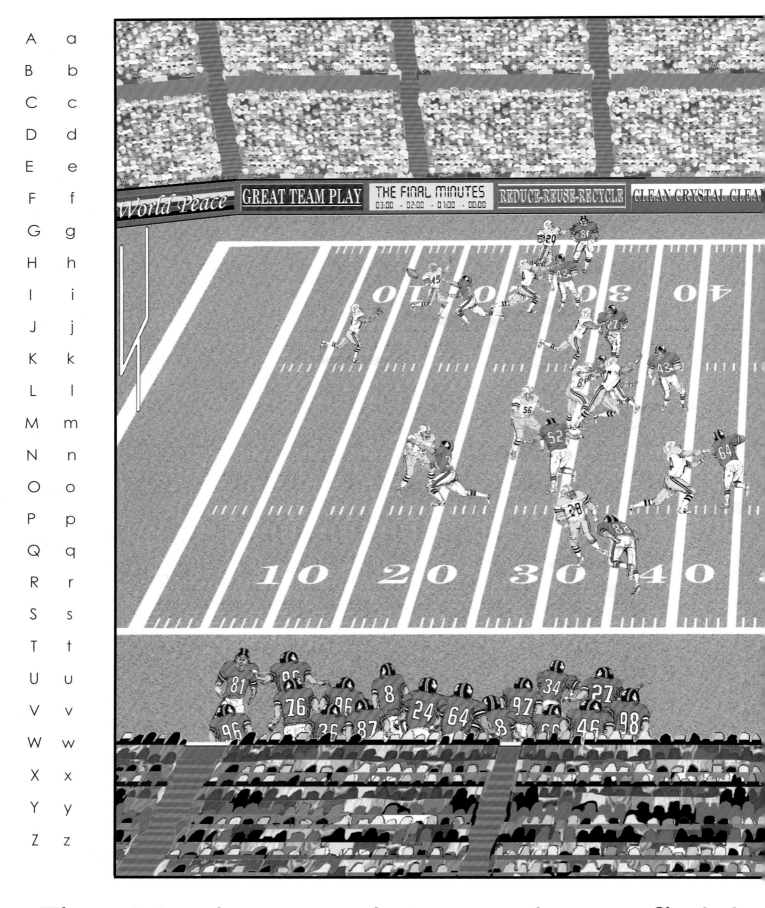

The Mustangs charge down-field following the high flying kick.

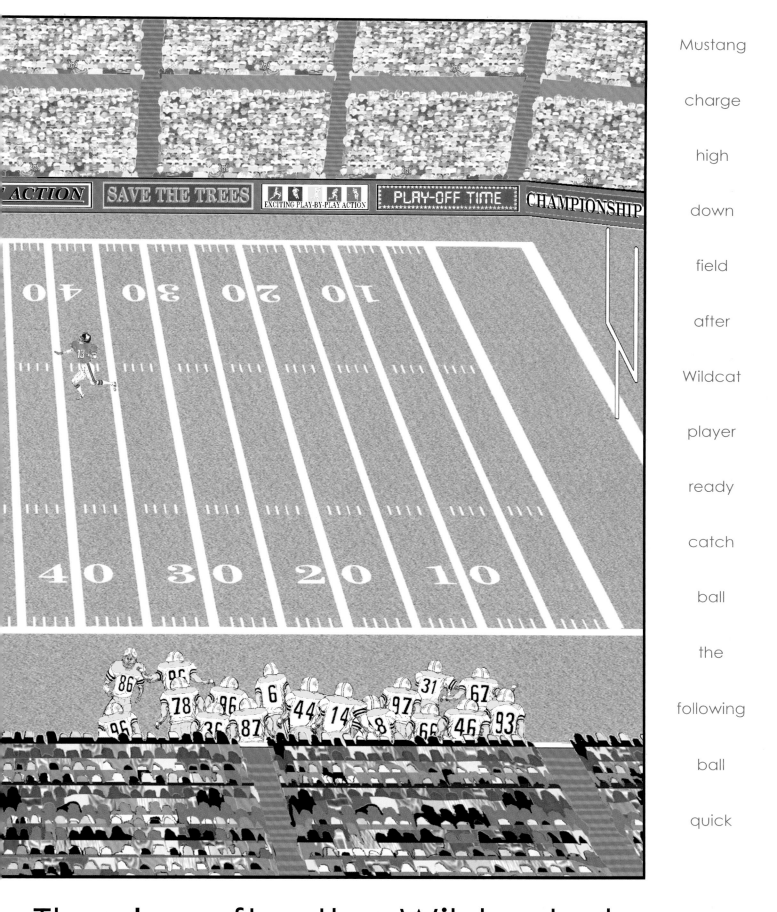

Mustang charge high down field after Wildcat player ready catch ball the following ball quick

They're after the Wildcat player who's ready to catch the ball quick.

A a
B b
C c
D d
E e
F f
G g
H h
I i
J j
K k
L l
M m
N n
O o
P p
Q q
R r
S s
T t
U u
V v
W w
X x
Y y
Z z

The fans cheer the great kick
with a thunderous roar.

fans cheer kick great thunderous roar with as Mustang tacklers the surround twenty four number

As the Mustang tacklers surround number twenty-four.

A a
B b
C c
D d
E e
F f
G g
H h
I i
J j
K k
L l
M m
N n
O o
P p
Q q
R r
S s
T t
U u
V v
W w
X x
Y y
Z z

© C.HICKS/2001

He catches the football and
drives straight ahead,

catches drives the football straight and he crashing ahead into wall red white of blue

crashing into a wall of
white, blue and red.

A a
B b
C c
D d
E e
F f
G g
H h
I i
J j
K k
L l
M m
N n
O o
P p
Q q
R r
S s
T t
U u
V v
W w
X x
Y y
Z z

The Wildcats have the ball
and are all set to go.

Wildcats the ball have and all are set go across Mustangs their linemen in row

Across are the Mustangs,
their linemen in a row.

A   a
B   b
C   c
D   d
E   e
F   f
G   g
H   h
I   i
J   j
K   k
L   l
M   m
N   n
O   o
P   p
Q   q
R   r
S   s
T   t
U   u
V   v
W   w
X   x
Y   y
Z   z

The quarterback hands off the
ball to his halfback.

quarterback
running
back
hands
off
big
his
center
and
guards
off
fend
as
the
attack

As the center and guards
fend off the attack.

A a
B b
C c
D d
E e
F f
G g
H h
I i
J j
K k
L l
M m
N n
O o
P p
Q q
R r
S s
T t
U u
V v
W w
X x
Y y
Z z

Turning up-field with
a deke and a feign.

12

up-field

turning

deke

with

and

feign

only

pounced

to

be

very

little

for

gain

on

Only to be pounced on for very little gain.

A a
B b
C c
D d
E e
F f
G g
H h
I i
J j
K k
L l
M m
N n
O o
P p
Q q
R r
S s
T t
U u
V v
W w
X x
Y y
Z z

©C.HICKS/2001

The quarterback waits, letting
some time tick away,

waits

quarterback

time

letting

some

tick

away

Wildcat

as

the

linebackers

anxious

are

to

play

as the Wildcat linebackers
are anxious to play.

They rush to get the Wildcat,
who fires a quick pass.

rush

Wildcat

to

get

fires

quick

pass

knock

ball

down

they

batting

the

grass

it

They knock down the ball,
batting it to the grass.

17

A   a
B   b
C   c
D   d
E   e
F   f
G   g
H   h
I   i
J   j
K   k
L   l
M   m
N   n
O   o
P   p
Q   q
R   r
S   s
T   t
U   u
V   v
W   w
X   x
Y   y
Z   z

"DEFENSE - DEFENSE!" The fans shout out really loud.

defense

the

shout

fans

out

loud

really

words

crowd

echo

in

"DEFENSE - DEFENSE!" The words echo in the crowd.

A a
B b
C c
D d
E e
F f
G g
H h
I i
J j
K k
L l
M m
N n
O o
P p
Q q
R r
S s
T t
U u
V v
W w
X x
Y y
Z z

He is back to pass, after the ball is snapped.

back he to pass after is ball snapped the pressure feeling surrounded he's and trapped

Feeling the pressure, he's surrounded and trapped.

The fans rise as the ball sails
to a man going deep.

fans

rise

as

ball

sails

man

deep

going

twenty

four

intercepts

pass

timing

leap

great

Twenty-four intercepts the pass,
timing his great leap.

The Mustangs have the ball, holding still in their stance.

ball

have

Mustangs

holding

still

stance

their

need

touchdown

win

have

chance

they

and

still

They need a touchdown to win,
and still have a chance.

A a
B b
C c
D d
E e
F f
G g
H h
I i
J j
K k
L l
M m
N n
O o
P p
Q q
R r
S s
T t
U u
V v
W w
X x
Y y
Z z

© C. HICKS / 2001

The quarterback takes the ball, looking for an open man.

quarterback ball takes open looking for man sprinting from tacklers as fast can he as

Sprinting from the Wildcat tacklers, as fast as he can.

© C. HICKS/2001

Scrambling, he sees number thirty-two, no way he will quit.

28

sees

scrambling

number

thirty

two

no

way

he

quit

finds

receiver

throws

just

as

hit

He finds his receiver and
throws, just as he is hit.

World Peace

CLEAN CRY

©C. HICKS/2001

The fullback catches the ball,
twisting quick and turning.

FAST ACTION

catches

fullback

ball

twisting

quick

turning

tacklers

dive

for

legs

his

fast

pumping

and

churning

The tacklers dive for his legs, pumping fast and churning.

A a
B b
C c
D d
E e
F f
G g
H h
I i
J j
K k
L l
M m
N n
O o
P p
Q q
R r
S s
T t
U u
V v
W w
X x
Y y
Z z

© C. HICKS/2001

Wow! That timely pass and catch keep the Mustangs alive.

that

wow

timely

pass

catch

keep

Mustangs

alive

set

next

game

ending

play

drive

this

They are set with the next play
of this game ending drive.

The Mustang drops back as the dome fills with loud noise.

drops

back

Mustang

dome

loud

fills

with

noise

aims

throws

ball

stepping

up

great

poise

He aims and throws the ball,
stepping up with great poise.

A a
B b
C c
D d
E e
F f
G g
H h
I i
J j
K k
L l
M m
N n
O o
P p
Q q
R r
S s
T t
U u
V v
W w
X x
Y y
Z z

©C.HICKS/2001

The Mustang catches it, to the cheer of thundering sounds.

Mustang

the

catches

cheer

it

thundering

sounds

ball

for

his

stretched

dragging

feet

stay

in-bounds

©C.HICKS/2001

He stretched for the ball, dragging his feet to stay in-bounds.

A a
B b
C c
D d
E e
F f
G g
H h
I i
J j
K k
L l
M m
N n
O o
P p
Q q
R r
S s
T t
U u
V v
W w
X x
Y y
Z z

The Wildcat endzone is down-field, thirty-five more yards.

endzone

down

field

thirty

five

yards

more

shouting

signals

out

back

stands

his

of

guards

Shouting out signals, the Mustang stands back of his guards.

© C.HICKS/2001

The excitement builds, as the
Wildcats charge in real rough.

builds
excitement
charge
as
Wildcats
real
in
rough
the
quarterback
throws
linemen
them
block
tough

The quarterback throws, as his linemen block them so tough.

A a
B b
C c
D d
E e
F f
G g
H h
I i
J j
K k
L l
M m
N n
O o
P p
Q q
R r
S s
T t
U u
V v
W w
X x
Y y
Z z

©C.HICKS/2001

Number eighty-four races past two defensive backs,

eighty

four

number

past

races

two

defensive

backs

football

reaching

leaves

he

them

his

tracks

reaching for the football, as he leaves them in his tracks.

A a
B b
C c
D d
E e
F f
G g
H h
I i
J j
K k
L l
M m
N n
O o
P p
Q q
R r
S s
T t
U u
V v
W w
X x
Y y
Z z

Touchdown! He catches the ball as he soars high in the air.

catches

football

touchdown

air

soars

high

Mustangs

win

game

the

not

second

to

spare

with

Wow! The Mustangs win the game,
with not a second to spare.

A a
B b
C c
D d
E e
F f
G g
H h
I i
J j
K k
L l
M m
N n
O o
P p
Q q
R r
S s
T t
U u
V v
W w
X x
Y y
Z z

© C. HICKS / 2001

The Mustangs jump for joy,
a celebration has started.

They shout and pump their arms, as the Wildcats look downhearted.

Wow! What fun and excitement for the fans who came.
The Wildcats and Mustangs played an awesome game.

The players fought hard with no energy to spare.
In the heat of the battle they always played fair.

The players now walk about and greet one another.
They reach to shake hands showing respect for each other.

Yes, winning the championship is a sensation.
And, playing with sportsmanship wins admiration.

Football Player Positions

Offensive Players

When a team has possession of the football and are trying to move the football down the field to score a touchdown, these players are on the field playing the following positions.

Quarterback - The quarterback receives the football from the center when the football is snapped. He will take the football and then either run, hand it off or throw it to a teammate.

Center - The center will hike (snap) the football to his quarterback to start each play.

Guards - The right guard and the left guard line up beside the center and block the other team players during each play.

Tackles - The right tackle and left tackle line up beside the guards and block the other team players during each play.

Fullback - The fullback lines up behind the quarterback and will block, run with the football or sometimes catch the football.

Halfback - The halfback also lines up behind the quarterback and will block, run with the football or sometimes catch the football.

Wide-Recievers - The wide-recievers will run down the field to catch the football. They also will block on some plays.

Defensive Players

When a team does not have possession of the football and are trying to stop the other team from moving down the field to score a touchdown, these players are on the field playing the following positions.

Defensive Tackles - The right tackle and left tackle line up at the line of scrimmage and will tackle the player with the football.

Defensive Ends - The right and left defensive ends line up on the line of scrimmage and rush to tackle the quarterback or the player with the football.

Linebackers - The linebackers play behind the lineman (tackles and ends). They will try to tackle the player running with the football or try to intercept (catch) the football when the quarterback throws a pass.

Defensive Halfbacks - The defensive halfbacks will tackle players with the ball and try to catch or knock down passes thrown by the quarterback.

Safety - A safety plays behind all the defensive players from the middle. He will tackle players and try to intercept or knock down passes thrown by the quarterback.

The Mustang offense is all set to go, as they have the ball.

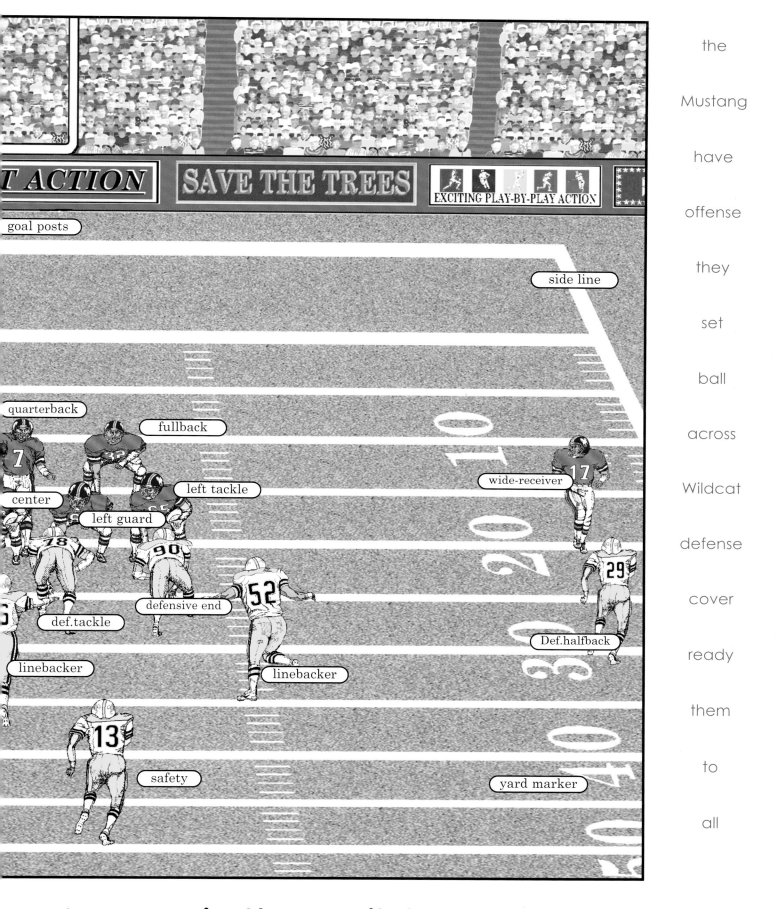

goal posts

side line

quarterback

fullback

wide-receiver

left tackle

center

left guard

def.tackle

defensive end

linebacker

linebacker

Def.halfback

safety

yard marker

the Mustang have offense they set ball across Wildcat defense cover ready them to all

Across is the Wildcat defense, ready to cover them all.

Football Glossary

Backs: The players who play away from the line of scrimmage, the halfback and the fullback on offense and the defensive backs on defense.

Ball carrier: Any player who has possession of the ball.

Blitz: A play where the defensive team sends players rushing towards the line of scrimmage as soon as the ball is snapped to try to sack (tackle) the quarterback.

Blocking: Offensive players preventing a defensive player from getting to the ball carrier. Blockers can use their arms and bodies but may not hold an opponent.

Center: The offensive lineman who hikes (snaps) the ball through his legs to the quaterback.

Complete pass: When the football is thrown forward to a teammate who catches it.

Down: A play or an attempt by the team on offense to gain 10 yards and recieve a new set of downs (plays)(American football has 4 downs, Canadian football has 3 downs)

Drive: The series of plays a team puts together in an attempt to score

Drop back: When a quarterback, after taking the snap, takes a few steps backward into an area called the pocket to get ready to pass the football.

End zone: The area between the end line and goal line, behind the goalposts, which a team on offense tries to enter to score a touchdown.

First down: The first play or attempt that a team on offense has to move 10 yards down the field, as soon as it gains 10 yards, it earns a new first down. (see above: down)

Goal line: A line drawn across the width of the field, which a team must cross with the ball to score a touchdown.

Hand-off: A running play where the quarterback hands the ball to a halfback or fullback.

In bounds: The region of the field inside the sidelines and end lines, where the game is played.

Interception: A pass caught in the air by a defensive player (team without the ball) whose team immediately gains possession of the ball and becomes the offense.

Kickoff: When a player kicks the ball to the opposing team, whose kick returner tries to run with the football the other way. (used to start the game, the second half after half time, and to restart play after each score.)

Line of scrimmage: An imaginary line where the the teams line up across from each other. No player may cross over until the ball is snapped.

Lineman: A player who starts each play within 1 yard of the line of scrimmage.

Open receiver: An offensive player who has no defensive player closely covering him.

Pass defender: A defensive player who covers an offensive receiver.

Pass protection: Blocking by the offensive players to keep the defensive players away from their quarterback on passing plays.

Pass rush: Defensive players rushing to get past blockers and sack (tackle) the quarterback.

Play: Action that begins with a snap of the ball and ends with the player with the ball being tackled to the ground.

Possession: When a player is holding or in control of the football, his team has possession.

Quarterback: The leader of the offensive players, he takes the snap from the center and either hands the ball to a back to run with it, passes it to a receiver or runs with the ball himself. He also communicates each play to his teammates.

Receiver: An offensive player who catches or attempts to catch a forward pass

Referee: The chief official; he makes all final decisions, acts as the timekeeper, calls any penalties and also starts and stops the action.

Rush: A running play; when a player runs with the football. Also a pass rush, when defensive players rush in to tackle the quaterback.

Sack: When the quarterback is tackled behind the line of scrimmage.

Scrambling: Evasive movements by a quarterback to avoid being tackled with the football.

Sideline: The boundary line that runs the length of the field along each side. A ball carrier or ball that touches or crosses the sideline is out of bounds and the play stops.

Snap: When the center crouches down and gets the signal from his quarterback, he quickly hands the ball between his legs to the quarterback standing behind him to start each play. (the ball is snapped)

Spiral: When a ball is thrown or kicked with a spin. The ball points in the same direction as it flys through the air. It will go faster and farther and is more accurate when it spirals.

Tackle: A player position on both the offensive and defensive lines. There is a left and right offensive tackle, and a left and right defensive tackle.
Also means to bring a player to the ground, stopping the play.

Tackling: Contacting a ball carrier to cause him to touch the ground with any part of his body except his hands, thereby ending the play.

Touchdown (TD): When a team crosses the opponent's goal line into the endzone with the ball, catches a pass in the opponent's end zone, or recovers a loose ball (fumble) in the opponent's end zone; this earns a team 6 points.

Literacy Guide

Practice early reading skills using the special page format.

The special page format is designed to enhance the opportunity for children to practice key skills in their reading development. The chart below highlights 4 specific skills that are fundamental building blocks required to produce a new reader. Along with the story text in black at the bottom of each story scene there are letters in blue on the left and words in red on the right as a quick and handy reference to practice some of these skills.

Use their current ability as a guide to focus on the appropriate skills to practice.

4 Building Blocks Of Reading - With Suggested Reading Skills Activities

Oral Language Development

Speaking aloud and expressing ideas and thoughts builds oral language skills and provides an essential foundation for the development of reading.

Suggested Activities

- look through the story letting the child talk and tell about the pictures using their own words

- encourage, listen and actively respond to the child's own words, thoughts and ideas

- prompt for more oral discussion and detail with questions and rephrasing their words and ideas

- take turns talking about the action and what the players and fans might be feeling, thinking and saying

Letter and Sound Recognition

An essential pre-reading skill is recognizing all the letters (upper and lower case) of the alphabet and the sounds that they make.

Suggested Activities

- together point to each blue letter, name and make the sound of each letter in the alphabet

- explain letters have a lower case (small) symbol and upper case (big) symbol

- name a letter, the sound it makes and then have your child point to it (take turns making it a fun game)

- identify a letter and see if it can be found in a red word on the left and in the story (letters make words)

Building Word Vocabulary

An important reading skill development is the ability to visually identify words, to recognize the grouping of letters and to remember the word meaning.

Suggested Activities

- point to and say a red word, name each letter and their sounds that group together making each word

- point to and read a red word and then let your child find it in the story sentence (take turns making it a game)

- take turns pointing to and reading aloud each red word from the top to bottom in order

- point to a red word, have your child say the word and explain it's meaning (make a sentence with the word)

Reading Fluency and Comprehension

Developing the ability to read words accurately and understand their meaning at the same time produces a fluent and competent reader.

Suggested Activities

- read the story together, develop a rythm and use the rhyme to create and model a natural reading fluency

- ask questions about the action and events to check for memory and understanding

- discuss the thinking, emotions and feelings of the many players and spectators watching the game

- talk about team work, fair-play and sportsmanship, allowing your child to express their feelings and ideas

Find a good balance between working with your child's current abilities and challenging them to learn!

Please support the literacy development of your child.